A GOOD THING HAPPENED TODAY

To my sources of good news: my two Christians,
Mamita, Dad, Joan & Nadir, and Quesnels up North
—M. F.

To Sebastian
—R. K.

A Good Thing Happened Today

Text copyright © 2022 by Michelle Figueroa

Illustrations copyright © 2022 by Ramona Kaulitzki

www.harpercollinschildrens.com

Library of Congress Control Number: 2021950881
ISBN 978-0-06-314231-2

The artist used Adobe Photoshop to create the digital illustrations for this book.
Typography by Rachel Zegar
22 23 24 25 26   PC   10 9 8 7 6 5 4 3 2 1
❖
First Edition

A GOOD THING HAPPENED TODAY

written by Michelle Figueroa

illustrated by Ramona Kaulitzki

HARPER

An Imprint of HarperCollinsPublishers

A good thing happened today.
Hooray! Did you hear?
Good things are happening every day
and everywhere!

When you look a little closer
you will surely find:
the world is mighty and loving,
and it is kind.

Some people bring water
to places without rain.

TSAVO, KENYA

Some people will sacrifice
so others can gain.

It doesn't take a lot
because goodness is free.

If you think outside the box,
good things happen—you'll see!

Like a library built
from discarded old books,

BOGOTÁ, COLOMBIA

books full of new wonder
and adventurous outlooks.

There is goodness we can't touch;
good that's not a "thing."

Good can be a moment

or a melody to sing.

Like songs played on cobblestone,
freely, off-the-cuff,

BOGOTÁ, COLOMBIA

for change, marbles, or smiles,
'cause love's payment enough.

We are never too young
and we are never too old,

to do good deeds,

to take a leap and be bold.

Whether it's a diploma

ITHACA, NEW YORK

or a kind letter,
tokens sealed with hope
can make our world better.

NETHERLANDS

Some good things happen
by a helping hand or two.

As long as someone's in need,
there's good left to do.

Like knitting old sweaters
into blankets—soft and warm.

Helpers help,

givers give,

and love weathers every storm.

When disaster strikes home,
and dark clouds make gray skies,

PUERTO RICO

good is a splash of color,
a seed of new life.

There's no need to search far,
close by there is good—
in every backyard
and in every neighborhood.

Good things can happen
inside your home, too,

as loved ones softly whisper,
"Good night, I love you!"

And where do good things come from?
They come from inside your heart.
Always choose to be kind . . .

'cause that's where good things start.

YOU ARE THE GOOD NEWS!

As a journalist, I have always been drawn to telling stories that showcase the good in humanity—I mean, humans are pretty amazing, right? I thought that not enough of these stories were being told, so I created Good News Movement on Instagram to showcase all those amazing humans (and animals) doing good things every day. People submit their own news, and I amplify their stories to millions that are part of our community and movement.

It's my mission to turn frowns into smiles, to inspire positive change, and to transform our landscape into one that acknowledges there's always more good than bad. I have found there is never a shortage of good news stories to tell.

My hope is that you, kind reader, realize that the good news isn't always somewhere else or happening to somebody else, but that you, yes YOU, are the good news and you can create positive impact. Whether it's helping a sibling, neighbor, your community, or changing the world—the good starts within you!

In this book, we share stories about a pea farmer in Kenya who drives hours to deliver water to thirsty animals in remote areas to help them survive droughts. Then we travel to Colombia, where an ingenious sanitation worker has collected over 25,000 books for his home library for all to visit, and he's donated countless books to schools. Then we bring you the story of one boy who offered all he had in his pocket so street musicians could play a love song for his mother. A grandfather graduates alongside his daughter, showing us one is never too old. You are never too young, either—a young girl in the Netherlands sends drawings to the elderly and those who feel lonely. A boy knits blankets out of old sweaters for those out in the cold. In Puerto Rico, after Hurricane Maria, kids come together to repaint homes and plant trees. There are kids right now selling lemonade to raise money to help others.

Good is happening now—I hope you find lots of it wherever you go!

—Michelle

BACKGROUND ON STORIES

In an effort to save wildlife, especially elephants, from dehydration during times of drought in Tsavo, Kenya, PATRICK KILONZO MWALUA has been delivering water to animals in the driest areas of his community for years.

Source: https://instagram.com/patrickmwalua?utm_medium=copy_link

JOSÉ ALBERTO GUTIÉRREZ, a garbage collector in Bogotá, Colombia, saved more than 25,000 discarded books over the course of twenty years, which now live in his at-home, open-to-the-public library called La Fuerza de las Palabras (The Strength of Words). He has donated hundreds of books to schools and founded the Fuerza de las Palabras Fundación, a foundation that encourages literacy, arts, and music throughout Colombia.

Source: *Digging for Words: José Alberto Gutiérrez and the Library He Built* by Angela Burke Kunkel, illustrated by Paola Escobar (Schwartz & Wade, 2020); ages 4–8

A young boy in Bogotá, Colombia wanted to show his mother how much he loved her, so he offered a quarter and some of his beloved marbles to a a group of musicians to play a song for his mama. Moved by the boy's gesture, the musicians played a song for his mother for free!

Source: www.instagram.com/p/CGK2ZUugWMk/?igshid=1lh32kmm8lv78

In 2018, at eighty-three years old, HERB DOIG graduated from Cornell University with a master's degree in natural resources. Making the day even more special, he graduated alongside his granddaughter KILEY MCPEEK, who earned her degree in applied economics and management.

https://news.cornell.edu/stories/2018/05/grandfather-and-granddaughter-graduate-together

During the COVID-19 pandemic, four-year-old LUNA of the Netherlands hand-delivered her homemade drawings to members of her community to cheer them up. The Dutch postal service sent her a custom-made blue-and-orange postal worker uniform and mailbag to help her with her deliveries!

Source: www.instagram.com/p/CJcX6PTM5aH/?igshid=wq9eabf6ru9o

After Hurricane Maria ravaged Puerto Rico in 2017, Samuel González rallied people to bring light back to their communities by removing debris and painting their neighborhoods vibrant colors. The bright, colorful neighborhoods, such as Aguadilla, helped stimulate tourism and rebuild Puerto Rico's economy.

Source: www.instagram.com/p/BtCynl2gpZt/?igshid=vyk0mfllvcb4